Dear Parent:
Your child's love of reading

Every child learns to read in a different way and at his or her own speed. You can help your young reader improve and become more confident by encouraging his or her own interests and abilities. You can also guide your child's spiritual development by reading stories with biblical values and Bible stories, like I Can Read! books published by Zonderkidz. From books your child reads with you to the first books he or she reads alone, there are I Can Read! books for every stage of reading:

SHARED READING
Basic language, word repetition, and whimsical illustrations, ideal for sharing with your emergent reader.

BEGINNING READING
Short sentences, familiar words, and simple concepts for children eager to read on their own.

READING WITH HELP
Engaging stories, longer sentences, and language play for developing readers.

READING ALONE
Complex plots, challenging vocabulary, and high-interest topics for the independent reader.

ADVANCED READING
Short paragraphs, chapters, and exciting themes for the perfect bridge to chapter books.

I Can Read! books have introduced children to the joy of reading since 1957. Featuring award-winning authors and illustrators and a fabulous cast of beloved characters, I Can Read! books set the standard for beginning readers.

A lifetime of discovery begins with the magical words **"I Can Read!"**

Visit www.icanread.com for information on enriching your child's reading experience.
Visit www.zonderkidz.com for more Zonderkidz I Can Read! titles.

"A foolish person lets his anger run wild.
But a wise person keeps himself under control."
— Proverbs 29:11

ZONDERKIDZ

The Mess Detectives and the Case of the Lost Temper
©2014 Big Idea Entertainment, LLC. VEGGIETALES®, character names, likenesses and
other indicia are trademarks of and copyrighted by Big Idea Entertainment, LLC. All
rights reserved.
Illustrations ©2011 by Big Idea Entertainment, LLC.

This title is also available as a Zondervan ebook.
Visit www.zondervan/ebooks.

Requests for information should be addressed to:

Zonderkidz, 3900 Sparks Drive, Grand Rapids, Michigan 49546

ISBN 978-0-310-74170-1

Editor: Mary Hassinger
Art direction: Karen Poth
Cover design: Ron Eddy
Interior design: Ron Eddy

Printed in China

14 15 16 17 18 19 /DSC/ 13 12 11 10 9 8 7 6 5 4 3 2 1

ZONDER**kidz**

I Can Read!

BEGINNING
READING
1

The Mess Detectives and The Case of the Lost Temper

story by Karen Poth

My name is Detective Larry.

This is my partner, Bob.

We solve mysteries.

Sometimes our jobs

are very messy.

Here is one of our stories.

It was a busy day.

Bob was in a bad mood.

We were looking for
the Masked Door Slammer.
We couldn't find him.

RINNNGGG!

A phone call came in.

It was Mr. Carrot.

"I heard a door slam,"

he said.

We drove to
the Carrot House.

When we got there

Bob's notebook was a mess.

That made him mad.

Mrs. Carrot came to the door.

"There's been a door slamming,"

Bob said.

"Yes! Mr. Carrot heard a door slam. He told us. But I didn't hear anything," said Mrs. Carrot.

"And I didn't hear anything," said Laura.

"We missed the door slammer,"
said Bob.

Bob was getting more upset.

"We have to get him,"
Bob said.
He got in the car.

We made a plan.

We would wear costumes

and sit outside the Carrot house

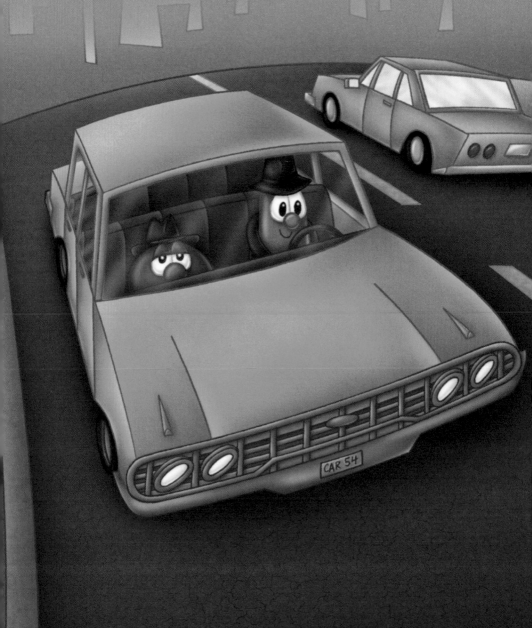

Bob put on his costume.

I put on my costume.

Bob said I had

the wrong kind of costume.

"You look silly!" Bob said.

He was getting more and more upset.

I was bored.

I didn't like waiting.

I got on my skateboard.

That made Bob really mad.
"We should be quiet,"
he said.

Then I did it.
I ordered a pizza.

Bob was so mad.
He was hopping all over.
Bob lost his temper!

"Bob, stop!" I said.

"You have lost your temper.

Just like the Masked Door Slammer."

Bob stopped to think.

"You're right, Larry," he said.

"I am sorry. It's not good to lose
your temper."

Just then we heard a door slam!

SLAMMM!

We ran inside.

"Where is he?" Bob asked.

"Who?" asked Laura.

SLAMMM!

"There it is again,"

Bob said.

"The Masked Door Slammer!"

We ran to the kitchen.

"I think it was the wind," said Laura.

"The wind slammed the door!"

Mystery solved!

Bob and I left the Carrot House.

Bob was smiling!

A foolish person lets his anger run
wild. But a wise person keeps
himself under control.

— Proverbs 29:11